Blueberry Pancakes

Written by Meg Caraher

Illustrated by Chris Lynch

sundance

a black dog book

Published by
Sundance Publishing
P.O. Box 1326
234 Taylor Street
Littleton, MA 01460

Copyright © text Meg Caraher
Copyright © illustrations Chris Lynch

First published 2000 by
Pearson Education Australia Pty. Limited
95 Coventry Street
South Melbourne 3205 Australia
Exclusive United States Distribution: Sundance Publishing

ISBN 0-7608-5014-3

Printed in China

Contents

Characters

Martin is
a good helper.

Anna is Martin's
bossy big sister.

Chapter One
Giant Hiccups

Anna is my sister. She's taller than I am.
I usually need her help to reach things
in high places. But not this morning.
This morning I could reach the ceiling.

When Mom and Dad went out,
they left Anna in charge.
I was doing my jigsaw puzzle.
I hiccupped, and the puzzle pieces
flew into the air.
So did I.

Hic-cup! Hic-cup! Another giant hiccup. They kept on coming.

"Anna! Help me!" I said. A huge hiccup sent me right over the top of her head.

"Martin!" said Anna. "This is awesome.
Mom and Dad left a list of jobs to do.
With your giant hiccups, we'll be done
in no time."

"I don't want to work," I said.

"I want to be . . . hic-cup! . . . cured."

Chapter Two
Hiccups at Work

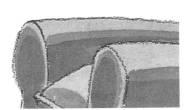

"Jobs first, cure later," said Anna.

"Job one—dust cobwebs.

Martin, stand under the cobwebs.

Hold a duster. And hiccup.

We won't need a ladder at all."

So I did. I hiccupped, and I dusted.
I dusted, and I hiccupped.

"Job two—hang out laundry.

Martin, hold the wet clothes.

Hiccup. And spin around in the air.

The clothes will dry extra fast.

We won't need a clothesline at all!"

So I did. I hiccupped, and I spun.

I hiccupped, and I dried.

I dried, and I spun, and I hiccupped.

"Job three—plant bulbs.

Martin, stand in the flower bed and hiccup.

You'll dig the holes when you land.

We won't need a shovel at all!"

So I did. I hiccupped, and I landed.

I hiccupped, and I dug.

I dug, and I landed, and I hiccupped.

The jobs were done. Finally Anna gave me
a big glass of water to cure my hiccups.

Chapter Three
My Reward

I drank all of the water in two huge gulps.
Hic-cup!

Anna told me to hold my breath.

I held it for as long as I could.

Hic-cup!

Hic-cup!

I was worn out from my giant hiccups.

I felt like they would never stop.

I needed to get my mind off the hiccups

and find a cure.

As a reward for all my work,
Anna cooked my favorite food.
Pancakes with blueberries
and whipped cream on top.

"Mmm. Excellent. Hic-cup!
Any more?" I asked.

Anna gave me a giant stack.

Then, hic-cup! I stacked the blueberries
on the pancakes.

"I'm building the biggest blueberry tower
on ... Hic-cup! ... Earth," I told Anna.

Splat!

Blue, squishy berries rolled everywhere.

Mom's white tablecloth turned berry-blue.

"Oh no! My tower!" I said.

Chapter Four
Hiccup Cure

"Oh no! My tablecloth!"

I got the fright of my life.
It was Mom. Home early.

I waited for a hiccup . . .

I looked at Mom's face.

It was terrifying.

I waited for a hiccup.

"Martin!" said Mom.

"What have you got to say for yourself?"

"I'm cured! No more hiccups!"

Then, I looked at the tablecloth.

"But," I said, "I have a funny feeling that I'll have more work to do!"